Harriet Strikes Again

Collins
R E D
STORYBOOK

Other Collins Red Storybooks

Simon and the Witch *Margaret Stuart Barry*
Disaster with the Fiend *Sheila Lavelle*
The Dancing Bear *Michael Morpurgo*
The Enchanted Horse *Magdalen Nabb*
Help! It's Harriet *Jean Ure*

Harriet
Strikes Again

Jean Ure
Illustrated by Stephen Lee

CollinsChildren'sBooks
An Imprint of HarperCollinsPublishers

First published in Great Britain by
CollinsChildren'sBooks 1996

1 3 5 7 9 8 6 4 2

CollinsChildren'sBooks is a division of
HarperCollins*Publishers* Ltd
77–85 Fulham Palace Road
Hammersmith, London W6 8JB

Text © Jean Ure 1996
Illustrations copyright © Stephen Lee 1996

The author and illustrator assert the moral right to be
identified as the author and illustrator of the work.

Printed and bound in Great Britain by
Caledonian International Book Manufacturing Ltd, Glasgow G64

ISBN 0 00 675151 2

CONTENTS

Harriet and the Ancient Remain   7

Help the Aged   31

What the Butler Saw   56

Harriet and the Hound from Hell   84

HARRIET AND THE
ANCIENT REMAIN

Harriet and Stinky Allport were digging a hole. A deep hole. Not quite as deep as all the way to Australia, but deep enough to stand up in.

They were digging it at the end of Stinky's garden, behind the vegetable patch where they couldn't be seen. In Harriet and Stinky's experience, it was always wisest to do things where you couldn't be seen. Grown-ups were full of the most peculiar and unreasonable prejudices. A large, deep hole lurking behind the vegetable patch might seem quite delightful to Harriet and Stinky, but who knew what a grown-up would make of it?

"They'd be just as likely to go raving mad,"

said Stinky. "Start on about how you've gone and dug up something valuable."

"There isn't anything valuable," said Harriet. "It's just earth."

"That's all you know," said Stinky.

"I put it to you," said Harriet. She stood, trowel in hand, hands on hips. "What's valuable about earth?"

"I dunno… could be special sort of earth."

"Well, it isn't. It's just earth. Get on and dig."

Stinky sighed. It was all very well for Harriet. This wasn't her garden and the grown-ups that were likely to go raving mad weren't her parents.

"Dig!" screamed Harriet.

Harriet dug with her trowel; Stinky dug with a shovel. The trowel was too small and the shovel was too bendy, but it was all they had. Stinky's dad had meanly put a padlock on the door of the garden shed after Harriet and Stinky had taken the garden hose out and accidentally drenched the next door neighbours, who had complained.

The trowel and shovel had come from Harriet's house; they were all she had been able to find. Harriet's dad, for some strange reason, had locked his garden shed as well. Harriet couldn't think why. It was hardly her fault if a can of paint had fallen on top of his flower pots and broken them. What had the flower pots been *doing* there? Right in the middle of the floor. Stupid place to keep flower pots, 'specially if you were going to have great heavy cans of paint balanced just above them.

She started to say as much to Stinky, but Stinky was just about sick of Harriet and her story of the flower pots. If she hadn't gone and smashed them her dad wouldn't have locked his garden shed and they could be digging with a proper spade and fork, instead of a ridiculous hand trowel and a bendy shovel.

"Never get anywhere at this rate!"

"Don't whinge," said Harriet.

"Why not?" said Stinky. "You were."

"I was not!"

"Oh yes you were! You were whingeing about your dad."

"I wasn't whingeing about *digging*."

"Well, but I can't work with this shovel," grumbled Stinky. "It bends."

"Oh, give it here!"

Harriet threw down her trowel and snatched impatiently at the shovel. For a few minutes, they dug in silence. They had been at it all morning and so far had nothing to show for it but a series of small, deep holes dug by Harriet (she tended to get bored working on the same one all the time) and a bucket-sized pit dug by Stinky, who was more orderly in his methods. The idea, explained Harriet, was that in the end, "We'll join them up and make one big one."

And then they could live in it. Not all the time, of course; just during school holidays or when life at home became more than usually unbearable, such as, for instance, when Stinky's cousin Giles came to stay and Stinky's mum kept telling everyone what a dear little boy he was, what wonderful manners he had and how she wished Stinky could be a bit more like him. That was when Stinky was going to go and live in the hole.

Harriet was going to live in it whenever her mother turned nasty. She had turned nasty just the other day, carrying on like a lunatic about the state of Harriet's bedroom.

"Said it was a pigsty!" Harriet set about, indignantly, with her bendy shovel. "Went on and on and *on* about it."

Harriet had been going on and on and on about it, too. Harriet tended to go on about things. If it weren't cans of paint being left where they could fall on top of flower pots, it was her mum having a go at her about her bedroom. This was at least the fifth time Stinky had heard the tale.

"I said to her," said Harriet, "it's *my* bedroom. And anyway, I happen to like pigs."

"Not indoors," said Stinky.

Harriet turned on him. "Who said anything about them being indoors?"

"You said your mum said your bedroom was like a pigsty."

"I didn't say there was a pig in it! Did I?'

Stinky squatted with his trowel, jabbing at the earth. "Can't think what else'd live in a pigsty."

"Are you calling me a pig?" shrieked Harriet.

"I thought you liked pigs."

"Oh, shut up!" said Harriet. "Get on digging."

When the hole was deep enough they were going to cover the floor with some old lino that Stinky's mum had thrown out and make a roof with plastic sheeting. They were going to have to buy the plastic sheeting, but they both agreed it would be worth it.

"It'll be a refuge for battered children," said Harriet, "same as they have for battered wives. And we'll put up a notice saying 'Private. No Trespassers'."

"Yeah, and 'Knock Before Entering'."

"And we'll keep cans of Coke and stocks of food and things to do."

"And something to sit on," urged Stinky, who liked to be comfortable. "We'll make it like a real house."

Before it could be like a real house it had to be dug deep enough for them to stand up in. There was a long way to go...

By tea time, when they had dug for four and a half hours, there was still a long way to go. A very long way. Their backs were aching and their hands were sore.

"It's going to take weeks at this rate," said Harriet.

Stinky was alarmed. He couldn't wait weeks! Goody-goody Giles was coming next weekend. The hole had to be dug by then.

"Well, I'm not digging any more today," said Harriet. "I'm tired. I'm going home to have my tea."

"See if you can get into your dad's garden shed and get a proper spade and fork," said Stinky.

"See if you can get into yours!" retorted Harriet.

It wasn't any use: Harriet couldn't get into the garden shed. Dad had put a padlock on it and hidden the key.

"I'm not having you kids," he said,

"messing about with my tools."

Harriet's sister Lynn said loftily that she never went anywhere near his tools, thank you very much. Harriet said neither did she, and it wasn't her fault if people went and left cans of paint dangerously balanced on the edges of shelves waiting to fall on top of flower pots.

Her dad said that was quite enough of Harriet's smart mouth and that Harriet shouldn't have been in the garden shed in the first place.

"And that is that. Flat and final. My last word on the subject."

Harriet's mum then said, "Yes, and what about that bedroom of yours? I thought I told you to tidy it up?"

Harriet said, "I did tidy it. I can't put everything away or I won't know where it is."

"Well, if it's still a pigsty by the weekend," said Harriet's mum, "that will be a second week without any pocket money."

They had to get that hole finished! But how?

Next morning, Stinky said gloomily, "So

you didn't manage to get in there, then?"

"Doesn't matter! I've had an idea. We don't need spades and forks," said Harriet. "We can get other people to dig for us!"

Stinky digested Harriet's idea in silence. It seemed to him there was a flaw in it.

"How'd we get 'em to do that?" he said.

"Easy!"

Harriet always had the answer to everything. "We just put up a notice. 'Historical Site. Ancient Remains.' Then everyone'll come flocking 'cause they'll think they might find something valuable."

"But there isn't anything valuable," said Stinky. "It's just earth."

"How do you know?" said Harriet.

"'Cause you said so," said Stinky. "Yesterday. You said it was just earth."

"Yes, and you said it might be special earth!"

"Well, that's what I thought but it obviously isn't. All that digging," said Stinky, "and we didn't find a thing, hardly. Just an old tin can."

"That's it!" said Harriet. "That's the remains!"

"Remains of what?"

"*Ancient* remains."

"Doesn't look very ancient to me." Stinky prodded at the can with his trowel. "Looks like it might have come from Sainsbury's."

"You only think that 'cause you're ignorant. You don't know how to tell. Could be from the Stone Age for all you know. That'd make it ancient remains."

"Ancient remain," said Stinky. "Remains is more than one."

"One's enough," said Harriet. "We could bury it right deep down so's they won't discover it till the hole's practically dug. Or wait till it is practically dug and then discover it ourselves."

"Maybe we ought to put in a bit of buried treasure to sort of encourage them," said Stinky. "I've got some old pennies upstairs – we could put them in. They're not worth anything."

"All right," said Harriet. "Let's go and get them and write out a notice."

They wrote out several notices, all neatly printed in their best hand.

Historical Sight
Ancent Remane
and Berrid Tresure
Come and dig!!
(Bring own tools)

At the foot they stuck one of Stinky's mum and dad's address labels and added the words, 'Come to back gate'.

"Now we'll go and fix them on lamp posts and things," said Harriet. "Get some Sellotape!"

After they had fixed the notices on lamp posts all up and down the road they went back to their hole to wait. They did a little digging, but not very much. Stinky scattered his old pennies and Harriet rubbed the tin can in the compost heap to try and make it look properly ancient. Then they settled back confidently to await the arrival of the diggers.

The first one to turn up was Wendy Williams, carrying what looked like a toy spade.

"Is this it?" she said pointing at the hole.

"Yes," said Harriet. "That is it."

"And it's really and truly got ancient remains in it?"

"Remain," said Stinky. "And buried treasure."

Wendy looked at him, challengingly. "How do you know?"

Stinky opened his mouth, but Harriet firmly stepped in. She wasn't having any of that sort of nonsense.

"It's a historical site. It's bound to have things in it. And anything you dig up," she added, "is yours to keep."

"So I should hope," said Wendy. "Not going to all the trouble of digging things up just for someone else, am I?"

Salim Khan was the next to arrive. Salim was carrying a proper fork and bucket, and looked as if he meant business.

"What's the bucket for?" said Harriet.

"To take away the treasure and the remains."

"Remain." Stinky said it weakly. He was beginning to foresee that there might be trouble.

Other people began to arrive – Gerry Mander and Hake-Face Heneghan with garden spades almost bigger than they were, Alison Leary and Snobby Clark with rubber gloves and a dustpan and brush because Alison (who always knew everything) said that when you were on historical digs you didn't *dig*, you brushed and swept and, "felt with your fingers. Otherwise you could ruin things. And historical isn't spelt like you've spelt it, and neither is buried and neither is treasure."

"Yes, and you mean site spelt s-i-t-e, not sight like you've got it," said Snobby.

Harriet would have liked to say something rude but she needed them to help with the hole, so she simply stretched her lips into a sickly smile and said, "You might as well be in charge as you know so much about it."

"That's probably a good idea," said Alison. "I'll direct the digging. If anyone finds anything, they must come to me."

"If I find anything," said a red-haired girl whose name Harriet didn't know, "I'm keeping it. And I jolly well better had find something," she added, in threatening tones. "I didn't come here just for the fun of it."

Harriet had met the red-haired girl before. She had turned up at a beautiful baby competition that Harriet had organised and had been nothing but a disagreeable nuisance.

"Some people," said Alison, rather loudly, to Snobby, "obviously do not understand the purpose of a historical dig. We are hoping to uncover important artefacts whose rightful place will be in the British Museum."

There was a silence.

"Historical what?" said Hake-face.

"Artichokes, or something." The red-head was already down on her knees, tunnelling furiously with a trowel and a hand fork. "Don't take any notice of her, she's batty."

Alison breathed, deeply. "Objects that we uncover will not belong to us. They'll belong to the Crown."

"Who says?"

"I do!"

"And who are you when you're at home?"

"I am in charge of this dig," said Alison.

"Yeah, and I'm a blue banana!" The red-head was scattering earth in all directions.

A flying gobbet hit Harriet in the eye. Stinky looked at her, helplessly. The dig had only just begun and already it was out of control!

Slowly, and with great dignity, Harriet rose to her feet.

"This garden is Stinky's garden and

whatever anyone finds belongs to Stinky. *But –*" she said it hastily, before the red-head could start throwing more earth at her – "Stinky has very generously decided that whatever anyone finds he's going to let them keep."

"That's not the law!" shouted Alison.

"It is in this garden," said Harriet.

By lunch time the hole was really beginning to look like a hole. Several people had dug up old pennies, Hake-face had found an interesting stone which he thought might be a fossil and Wendy had uncovered a house brick.

There had been great excitement over the house brick. Alison and Snobby had gone rushing over with their dustpan and brush, screaming at Wendy not to touch it in case it might be an ancient remain. They now thought that probably it wasn't, but it had given them all fresh hope and the determination to carry on.

"After all, we haven't really found anything yet," said the red-haired girl. "I don't call a few old pennies buried treasure. And I don't call a mouldy old house brick ancient remains, either."

"Remain," said Stinky, feebly.

The girl tossed her head. "Yes," she said, "I'm going to, and I'd just better find something!"

"You mean you're not going home for lunch?" said Harriet.

"I'm going to stay right here," said Red-head, "and dig till I find something. And if I don't –"

If she didn't, there would be trouble.

"Now what are we going to do?" whispered Stinky. They could hardly bury the Ancient Tin in full view of Red-head. "I knew this was a rotten idea!"

"You're crazy," said Harriet. "It's one of the best ideas I've ever had."

By the end of the afternoon the hole was going to be plenty big enough to stand up in. Tomorrow they could put down their lino and buy their plastic sheeting, and by the weekend they could take up residence. Mum could complain all she liked about Harriet's bedroom being a pigsty. Stinky's mum could praise Goody-goody Giles to the skies.

Harriet and Stinky would be tucked away in their underground home!

"She'll get really ratty," worried Stinky, "if she doesn't find anything."

"Think I care?" said Harriet.

"Just better be something," muttered Red-head.

Fortunately, there was. Alison found a piece of pottery which she was convinced was Roman, Hake-face dug up another fossil and someone else found an interesting-looking bone which was almost certainly prehistoric.

"Dinosaur or something, I shouldn't be surprised."

At the last minute, while everyone was busy admiring the prehistoric dinosaur bone, Harriet managed to bury the Ancient Tin. Stinky waited anxiously for Red-head to uncover it. Would an Ancient Tin satisfy her? Or would she throw a tantrum and say it came from Sainsbury's?

"Hey!" Red-head sat back triumphantly on her heels. "Look what I've got!"

Everyone turned to look. It wasn't the Ancient Tin, but a small blue bottle with a

glass stopper.

"That *has* to be ancient," said Harriet. "That is a really *good* find."

"Mm… it's all right, I suppose." Red-head, even now, tended to be grudging. "I don't expect it's worth much, but it's quite pretty." She held it up to the light. "I could always give it to my mum."

"*What* a nice idea," gushed Harriet.

"On the other hand," said Red-head, "I might decide to sell it. I might get given a fortune for it."

As they all trooped off carrying their bits of Roman pottery and prehistoric bones, Stinky said in worried tones, "You don't think she will, do you?"

"Will what?"

"Get given a fortune. I mean," said Stinky, "this is my garden. Everything in it's mine by rights. You said so."

"I said you'd very generously decided to let people keep whatever they dug up. *Honestly*," said Harriet, "you've got your hole. What more do you want?"

Next day they laid their lino and bought their plastic sheeting. Harriet was still lost in wonderment at her own brilliance. Without her they would never have had a hole!

"All it takes is a bit of brain power," she said.

That night, Stinky's dad walked down the garden to tip some vegetable peelings on the compost heap and fell feet first into the hole.

The following day, he stood guard over Harriet and Stinky while they filled the hole in again.

By tea time, Harriet and Stinky ached in

every bone in their bodies and the hole was no longer there.

Harriet's mum had stopped her pocket money for the second week running and Goody-goody Giles was due to arrive first thing Sunday morning.

"You and your brilliant ideas," said Stinky.

"I like that! Whose idea was it to dig a hole in the first place?"

"Yours," said Stinky.

"Humph!" said Harriet.

Dragging herself wearily home, Harriet bumped into Red-head.

"Hey, you know that Ancient Remain?" said Red-head. "Guess what? My mum took it down the antique shop and they gave us fifteen pounds for it!"

Life, thought Harriet, could be very bitter at times.

HELP THE AGED

One day in class Mrs Middleton said, "Tell me! How many of you ever travel by bus?"

Most people put their hands up.

"How many of you have ever travelled on a bus when it was full?"

A few of the hands went down.

"How many of you have ever given up your seat to an elderly person?"

A bit of wavering, eyes flickering sideways to see how other people were going to respond, then one by one the hands began to droop and fall until in the end not one single hand was still up.

"Hm!" said Mrs Middleton. "So how many of you would consider giving up your seat to an elderly person? If you happened to see an elderly person standing?"

Alison Leary's hand promptly shot into the air, straight and stiff like a flag pole. It was followed immediately by Snobby Clark's and then, rather more slowly, by Wendy Williams', Salim Khan's and one or two of the others.

Harriet sat frowning, trying to decide. *Would* she give up her seat to an elderly person? She might – but, then again, she might not. It would depend what the elderly person looked like. If she looked frail and fragile, then Harriet probably would. But if she looked like Miss Dunc up the road, then Harriet most definitely would not. Miss Dunc was short and stout and bristly, and totally disagreeable. Miss Dunc would deserve to stand.

In any case, if she put her hand up now it would seem as though she were just copying Alison Leary. Harriet folded her arms and stared defiantly straight ahead.

"Well!" said Mrs Middleton. "I'm glad to see that at least a few of you still know the meaning of good manners."

Alison's hand quivered self-righteously. Full of virtue, was Alison.

"What about the rest of you? Joseph! You're looking very militant. Why wouldn't you give up your seat?"

Joseph, better known as Hake-face, said that he reckoned he'd got just as much right to sit down as anybody else.

"I'd have paid my fare same as what they'd done."

"Yeah." Stinky Allport nodded. "I don't see why people should get special treatment just 'cause they're old."

"Specially when they're crabby," said Hake-face. "Always keeping on at you and telling you not to do things."

"Like, I was on this bus the other day," said Stinky, "and there was this old woman had a go at me just for breathing. It's all I was doing, just breathing. She said I was doing it down her neck, like I was doing it on purpose. Said it was creating a draught."

"I had this one said I trod on her foot deliberate," said Hake-face. "Said young people today didn't have no respect."

"I don't think old people have got respect," said Stinky. "They seem to reckon just 'cause you're young they can abuse you as much as they like."

"Well, all right, we've heard from the boys," said Mrs Middleton. "What about one of the girls? Harriet! Why the big scowl?"

The big scowl was for Alison Leary and her friend Snobby Clark, smugly sitting side by side with their haloes all polished and shining. Harriet bet no old person had ever told them off for creating draughts or treading on feet. Those two never did anything wrong.

"Come on, Harriet!" said Mrs Middleton. "Let's hear your views on the subject."

"What I think –" Harriet scraped her throat. "– is that if it was a nice old person I'd give them my seat, and if it was a cross old person I wouldn't."

Alison sniggered, as if Harriet had said something stupid. But other people nodded, and murmured their agreement.

"Yeah! If it was a nice old person."

"Not if it was a cross one."

"How can one tell?" wondered Mrs Middleton. "Can one tell just by looking?"

Harriet thought of Miss Dunc and decided that you probably could.

"If they look miserable " she pulled down the corners of her mouth.

"Yeah, like sometimes they smile at you and other times they look at you like you're some kind of mess, or something."

"Like they want to stamp on you."

"So you don't think," said Mrs Middleton, "that when people get old they deserve to have allowances made for them?"

The class considered the proposition.

"No," said Hake-face.

"Not if they're nasty," said Harriet.

"Ought to have allowances made for us, being young," said Stinky.

"Oh, you do!" said Mrs Middleton. "I assure you, you do!"

Stinky smirked, not quite certain how to take this.

"I think," said Mrs Middleton, "that I should like us all to consider how it might feel, to be old... to run out of energy, to have aches and pains, to be a bit stiff, a bit deaf, maybe not see too well. I think it might do some of us good. I know you probably can't imagine it at the moment, but you're all going to be old yourselves one day. Perhaps you might like to project yourselves into the future and think what you'll be like in sixty years' time."

Stinky jumped up and began to shuffle about the room, groaning loudly as he did.

"Exactly!" said Mrs Middleton. "Just think of that, when you're sitting on a bus and see old people standing. One of these days, it might be you!"

Harriet enjoyed the sort of game where you had to use your imagination and pretend to be someone different. She played the being-old game in the playground all through break along with Stinky and Hake-face and Wendy Williams. Then she played it again when she got home.

Old people, she thought, sometimes had trouble with their teeth which meant they had to slurp their food. Harriet slurped, gustily.

"Harriet!" cried her mum. "For heaven's sake! Keep your mouth closed when you're eating."

"I can't," said Harriet, dribbling a strawberry yoghurt all down her front. "I'm doing a project for school."

"A project on eating disgustingly?"

"Project on old people," said Harriet. "I'm eating like an old person."

"Rubbish!" snapped Mum. "When did you ever see your gran eat with her mouth open?"

Never, was the answer to that. Harriet's gran was very small and neat and trim. She wouldn't dream of dribbling yoghurt down herself.

"How old is Gran?" said Harriet.

"Sixty," said Mum.

"I'm being eighty," said Harriet.

After tea, she went upstairs to be eighty in

her bedroom. What was it Mrs Middleton had said? "How it might feel to be old... to run out of energy, to have aches and pains, to be a bit stiff, a bit deaf, maybe not see too well."

It wasn't going to be easy, but Harriet enjoyed a challenge. "Run out of energy." All right! She would jump up and down one hundred times on the spot. That should run her out of energy.

Harriet jumped. One! Two! Three! Four! She managed to get as far as ninety-two before her mum's voice came yelling up the stairs.

"Harriet! Stop that! You'll bring the ceiling down."

Really, her mum wasn't any help! This was a serious experiment. Harriet sank on to the bed, panting, to work out 'aches and pains.'

How could you give yourself aches and pains? Harriet thought about it. An idea came to her. She took her pencil sharpener out of her bag. The pencil sharpener was in the shape of a frog – all angles and pointy bits. Then she took off one of her shoes and stuffed the pencil sharpener right down into the toe. Then she put her foot back into the shoe and trod across the room.

Ow! Ooo! Ouch! That was pain, all right. Nobody could walk far with a pencil sharpener in her shoe.

She didn't know what to do about aches. In the end she pulled her long woolly school scarf out of a drawer and wound it round her middle as tight as it would go; so tight she could hardly breathe. It wasn't quite an ache and it wasn't quite a pain, but maybe it was what old people felt like when they had difficulty breathing. Mrs Middleton hadn't mentioned that one.

What was next? "A bit stiff." Hmm...

A ruler! A plastic ruler stuck through the tight scarf, making the tight scarf even tighter and the whole of Harriet's right side as stiff as a board. She couldn't bend up, she couldn't bend down, she couldn't bend sideways. You couldn't get much stiffer than that.

"A bit deaf" was easy: Harriet simply helped herself to two of Mum's cotton wool balls from the bathroom and stuffed them in her ears.

"Maybe not see too well." That was easy, too: one of Mum's gauzy scarves (borrowed from Mum's dressing table drawer) tied around her eyes. Now all she could see were faint shapes in the darkness, and the only sounds she could hear were muffled. Just like an old person!

All she needed was a walking stick. Where could she find a walking stick?

I know! thought Harriet. One of Dad's garden canes.

Stiff and aching, half blind and almost deaf, Harriet felt her way along the landing and hobbled down the stairs. The frog pencil sharpener dug into her foot, the plastic ruler jabbed her in the ribs. At the bottom of the stairs, she bumped into someone coming the other way.

"What are you doing?" shrieked Lynn.

"I'm being an old person," said Harriet.

"You look pathetic!"

Old people quite often looked pathetic. They were either thin as sticks or fat as bubbles or else completely shapeless. Harriet could have stuffed some pillows

down her sweater and been a fat one. Fat people waddled. Harriet waddled. Down the hall, out through the kitchen, into the garden, down the –

"Ouch!" yelled Harriet, tripping over an unseen obstacle and banging her head against something hard.

She tore off Mum's gauzy scarf and saw Fat Cat leaping away with his tail in the air.

"You did that on purpose!" bawled Harriet.

Next morning, Harriet limped her way in to school. She had a big red blister on one of her toes plus some very sore ribs where the ruler had jabbed at her. She also had a large ugly lump on the side of her head and a painful purple graze on one of her knees.

If this was how it felt to be an old person, then Harriet could quite understand how old people were sometimes a bit grumpy. In future she would go out of her way to be kind and considerate and do all that she could to help them.

Harriet spent the whole of Saturday morning trying to help old people. It wasn't always easy since some of them didn't seem to want to be helped. One old man became quite angry when Harriet attempted to drag him across to the other side of the road. He claimed he hadn't wanted to go there, but if that were the case, why had he been dillying about at the kerb? Harriet made allowances for him: he was obviously confused. It wasn't his fault if he couldn't remember where he wanted to go.

Another old person screamed that Harriet was trying to mug her – all because Harriet had offered to carry her shopping bag! And an elderly couple threatened to "call the police immediately if you don't go away and leave us alone". Harriet had only wanted to help load their shopping into the boot of their car for them.

Poor old people, with their aches and pains! They shouldn't have to do these things. But some old people, as Harriet was discovering, could be very stubborn.

She had just about decided to give up and go home when she saw a sweet old lady with snow white hair tottering towards her.

The sweet old lady was wearing a blue dress and bedroom slippers. (Bedroom slippers? In the street?)

"Little girl," said the old lady, "I wonder if you could spare a penny? I've been out since early morning. I would so love a cup of tea."

"You can't buy a cup of tea for a penny," said Harriet.

The old lady's face crumpled. She held out her hands, piteously.

"Then what am I to do?"

Harriet looked at the bedroom slippers. They were wet and dirty, as if the old lady had been treading in puddles.

"Haven't you got anywhere to go?" said Harriet.

"Nowhere!" A tear rolled down the old lady's cheek. "My daughter threw me out. She said I was a nuisance."

Harriet's heart swelled. How cruel people were!

"Would you like to come home with me?" she said. "I could give you a cup of tea."

"Could I stay with you?" said the old lady.

"Well–" Harriet hesitated. "I'd have to ask my mum about that. But I could give you some tea."

Harriet and the old lady walked home together. They went in the back way, through the kitchen door.

"You wait here," said Harriet. "I'll go and see where my mum is."

In the hall she met Lynn on her way out through the front.

"Dad's gone off to the football," said Lynn,

"and Mum's in the lounge talking to Miss Fanshawe."

"Oh!" Harriet knew Miss Fanshawe. She had once run a lucky dip for her at a church fete.

"You're not to go in there," said Lynn. "They don't want to be disturbed. Miss Fanshawe's very upset about something."

Yes, and she might get even more upset if she saw Harriet. Harriet had just remembered that there had been a little bit of a muddle over the lucky dip and Miss Fanshawe hadn't been very happy with her. It might be best if Harriet stayed away.

She went back to the kitchen and found that the sweet old lady had opened the refrigerator and taken out a big bowl of trifle that Harriet's mum had made specially for tomorrow, when Auntie Eileen and Uncle Roger were coming. The sweet old lady had trifle all round her mouth, over her fingers and down the front of the blue dress.

"Um -" said Harriet.

"This is very poor trifle," said the sweet old lady. She said it quite crossly. "There doesn't seem to be any sherry in it."

The old lady tossed what was left of the trifle into the sink. "Where's my cup of tea?"

"I'll put the kettle on," said Harriet.

"Earl Grey," said the old lady.

"Pardon?" said Harriet.

"I only drink Earl Grey."

Poor muddled old lady, thought Harriet. How could you drink a *person*? Harriet took out a mug and placed a Tetley tea bag in it.

"Why isn't the heating on?" said the poor muddled old lady. "I'm cold! I'll catch my death! Go and get me a cardigan."

Harriet scuttled to obey. You had to make allowances when people were old.

When she came back, with one of Lynn's cardigans (Lynn surely wouldn't mind, if it was helping a poor old lady?) the fridge was open again and a puddle of spilt milk lay across the floor.

"I want something to eat," said the old lady. "What have you got that I can eat?"

"Um... bread and butter?" said Harriet. "Biscuits? Cornflakes? Bag of crisps?"

The old lady didn't want any of those things. She wanted a decent meal, she said. Nobody ever gave her a decent meal.

"There's cake," said Harriet.

Grudgingly, the old lady accepted a slice of Mum's best fruit cake. Harriet made the tea and put it on the table.

"What's that?" said the old lady. "That's not Earl Grey!"

"It's all we've got," said Harriet.

"Well, I can't drink it. I only drink Earl Grey. And I can't eat this cake!" The old lady suddenly spat the cake out, all over the table. "Don't you have anything decent in this house?"

Pressing her lips tightly together, Harriet wiped the cake off the table with the kitchen sponge. The old lady had picked up Lynn's cardigan and was staring at it, fretfully.

"Man-made fibre! I can't wear man-made fibre!" She flung the cardigan across the room. "Cheap and nasty! I only wear wool."

"That cardigan belongs to my sister," said Harriet.

"Then your sister has very poor taste, that's all I can say. I really don't know why you invited me here if you can't look after me properly. When you ask a guest into your house, it is only common courtesy to offer her the best. Now I want to use the bathroom. Kindly direct me to the bathroom."

Harriet led the old lady upstairs. The old lady seemed sprightly enough. She didn't appear to have any aches or pains and she certainly wasn't blind or deaf, so there really wasn't any excuse for such unpleasant behaviour.

"I'll wait for you down in the hall," said Harriet.

Maybe she could smuggle the old lady back out before Mum discovered her. She was beginning to think that perhaps she had made a bit of a mistake, bringing her back for tea. But what was she to do with her? You couldn't just abandon an old lady on the streets, especially not an old lady in bedroom slippers.

As she stood in the hall she could hear Mum and Miss Fanshawe, talking. Miss Fanshawe was saying, "I don't mind her being difficult, but why –" Miss Fanshawe's voice broke – "why does she have to be so unkind to me all the time? Nothing I do is ever right for her. All she does is carp and criticise."

"There, there!" said Mum. "I'm sure you've done your best. Tell me again what happened."

Harriet heard Miss Fanshawe sniffing and blowing her nose.

"She threw her morning cup of tea at me and walked out. I didn't realise until about

an hour later that she'd gone. I thought –"
Miss Fanshawe started to weep again – "I
thought I'd let her stew in her own juice. I
thought it would teach her a lesson. If
anything happens to her, it will be all my
fault!"

"No, no," said Mum. "You mustn't
blame yourself."

"But she hasn't any coat!" wailed Miss
Fanshawe. "And she's only wearing bedroom
slippers!"

"Excuse me –" Harriet opened the door
and poked her head round.

"Not just now, Harriet! Miss Fanshawe
and I are talking. Please go away."

"But, Mum –"

"Harriet! Did you hear what I said?"

"Yes, but M–"

"*Mother!*" Miss Fanshawe suddenly leapt
from her chair and sprang across the room.

"Oh, there you are," said the old lady. "I
wondered where you'd got to. This is a
terrible house, they haven't any Earl Grey…"

"Oh, Mother, really!" said Miss Fanshawe.

"*Harriet?*" said Mum.

"I found her," said Harriet. "Outside the supermarket."

"And you recognised her," cried Miss Fanshawe, "and brought her home! Oh, what a good, kind child you are! I can't tell you how relieved I am! Let me give you a little something in token of my gratitude."

Miss Fanshawe took out her purse and counted out five pound coins.

"I hope you don't mind loose change," she said.

Harriet turned, wide-eyed, to her mum.

"Is it all right?" she said.

"Of course it is!" said Miss Fanshawe. "Take it, with my blessing! If only there were a few more children like you around, the world would be a better place."

One hour later, Harriet sauntered back into town looking for something to spend her five pounds on. There didn't seem to be quite so many old people around as there had been in the morning, and that was just as well because Harriet had rather gone off the idea of helping them.

As she approached the shopping mall she met Stinky Allport.

"Hi," said Stinky.

"Hi," said Harriet.

They wandered on together.

"Look," said Stinky. "They've set up the Space Ball."

"Hake had a go at that," said Harriet. "It made him feel sick."

"Wouldn't make me feel sick," boasted Stinky.

"Wouldn't make me feel sick," said Harriet.

"If we had some money," said Stinky, "we could have a go on it."

"I've got money." Harriet pulled out her purse. As she did so, a smiling old lady thrust a collecting tin at her. On the tin it said 'Help the Aged'.

"I've got five pounds," said Harriet.

"We could have two goes for that," said Stinky.

The smiling old lady rattled her tin.

"Help the aged," she said.

Harriet and Stinky walked on.

"Else we could have just one go and spend

the rest on something else," said Stinky. "Like we could go to McDonald's or –"

Stinky broke off as Harriet suddenly stopped.

"What's the matter?" said Stinky.

Harriet heaved a deep sigh. "Bother," she said.

Stinky watched in disbelief as Harriet walked back to the old lady and dropped a pound coin in her collecting tin.

"What d'you go and do that for?" he said.

"I dunno," said Harriet. "Just felt like it, I s'pose."

What the Butler Saw

Harriet was short of money. It was nothing new: Harriet was often short of money. But on this occasion she was desperate. She needed thirty-three pounds and she needed it in a hurry. One of the shoe shops in town was having a sale, and in the sale was a pair of super de luxe Olympic trainers with red tabs, reduced from fifty pounds to thirty-five pounds. A bargain!

The only problem was, Harriet didn't have thirty-five pounds. She didn't even have five pounds. All she had, left over from her birthday, was a book token worth three pounds and some twenty-pence pieces which she had been keeping in a plastic tube that had once contained Easter eggs.

She said to her sister, "You wouldn't lend me thirty-three pounds, would you?"

She knew that Lynn had far more than that in her building society account, because Lynn was saving for a pair of ice skates. She could easily have taken out a bit to lend to Harriet, but of course she wouldn't.

"You must be joking," she said.

It was what she always said when Harriet asked her for anything.

"I'm not joking," said Harriet. "I'm serious."

"So am I," said Lynn. "That money is earning *interest*. Are you going to pay me interest?"

"Will if you like," said Harriet.

Lynn tossed her head.

"Pigs might fly!" she said, whatever that was supposed to mean.

What it meant was that Lynn did not intend lending Harriet any money.

"Not now, not tomorrow, not ever!"

It was terrible to have a sister who was

so stingy, but then her parents were pretty stingy, too. It obviously ran in the family; they were all stingy except Harriet. Harriet would gladly have lent her book token to anyone who wanted it. They only had to ask.

When Harriet tried asking – "Mum, you couldn't lend me thirty-three pounds, could you? For my trainers?" – all her mum said was, "You've already got a perfectly good pair of trainers! What do you want another pair for?"

Harriet tried explaining how these were special trainers, de luxe Olympic trainers with red tabs, but Mum remained unmoved.

She said, "I'll buy the book token off you, but I'm certainly not giving you thirty-three pounds."

"I don't want you to give it me," said Harriet. "Just lend it."

"Where's the difference?" said Mum.

Imagine having a mother who didn't know the difference between giving and lending!

Harriet's dad wasn't much better. He said,

"Harriet, if I were made of money I would give it you gladly. As I'm not, I'm afraid you'll have to manage without."

"I only want to borrow it," said Harriet.

"Borrow?" said her dad. He gave a hollow laugh. "That's a good one!"

It was amazing to Harriet that they couldn't find thirty-three pounds just to lend their own daughter. They didn't seem to mind paying out small fortunes on other people.

On Saturday, for instance, a man was coming to stay. He was coming for lunch and for supper and sleeping overnight.

Neither Mum nor Dad had ever met him before but Mum was all in a flap about whether the spare bed was going to be comfortable enough, and whether they ought to buy a new duvet and a new duvet cover, and what they were going to give him to eat.

Ordinary food wasn't good enough for Tristram de Vere. Tristram de Vere was a *professor*. He couldn't be expected to eat spaghetti hoops or baked beans on toast.

Mum had to go to Sainsbury's and buy all kinds of exotic stuff like egg plants and avocados, and passion fruit and mango, and sherry and wine and a bottle of whisky in case he was a drinker.

Why couldn't professors eat ravioli or jam pudding? Mum said in shocked tones that you couldn't offer ravioli and jam pudding to a guest (though it was perfectly all right to offer it to your daughter).

She said that Professor de Vere was coming all the way from London and deserved special treatment. He had been invited by the local history society, of which Mum and Dad were members.

He was going to give a lecture, with slides, on the subject of 'Life Below Stairs in Victorian England'. Mum was really looking forward to it.

"What's life below stairs?" said Harriet.

She thought perhaps it might be something to do with people living in cupboards, but Dad said it was "Servants, living in the basement. In the days when people *had* basements."

That was a pity! It would be far more interesting to live in a cupboard.

Harriet had often considered the possibility of moving into the cupboard under the stairs and making it into her own private house, with carpet and furniture and a proper knocker on the door. Living in a cupboard would be a challenge: anyone could live in a basement.

"Won't it be rather boring?" she said.

"Probably," said Dad.

"Oh, Tony, it won't!" cried Mum. "It'll be fascinating! I'm really excited by it."

Dad wasn't excited but he had to go along to work the projector: Professor de Vere was nervous of technology.

"He says he always manages to put the slides in upside down!" laughed Mum.

"Sounds a right yum-yum," said Dad.

Mum looked shocked.

"He's been on television," she said. "He's written books. He knows all there is to know about the Victorian period."

"So will people actually pay money to go and listen to him?" said Harriet.

"Amazingly," said Dad, at the same time as Mum said, "Of course they will! The hall's booked out."

"And all he's going to do is talk and show slides?"

"Isn't that enough?" said Mum.

Dad and Harriet looked at each other. Dad shrugged his shoulders. Harriet shook her head.

"Weird!" said Harriet.

Anyone could just talk and show slides. Harriet herself could talk nineteen-to-the-dozen. She frequently did so.

If only she had some slides...

That afternoon she went into town to look at her trainers. She had to keep checking that they were still there, even if she couldn't afford to buy them. There was one more week of the sale to go. What was she going to do? She had to have those trainers!

Harriet left the shoe shop, where the assistants were beginning to eye her suspiciously, and trundled gloomily out into the market. Most of the market was stalls selling fruit and veg and potted plants. Boring!

There was only one stall that Harriet ever looked at and that was

```
MICHAEL WREN
FRESH FROM
THE HEN
```

which once upon a time had sold free-range eggs and now sold an interesting clutter of old books and gramophone records and what Harriet's mum called "knick-knacks". Harriet never actually bought anything, but she always liked to stop and investigate.

"You again!" said Michael Wren.

So what? thought Harriet. There wasn't any law against just stopping to look, was there?

She lived in hope she might one day stumble upon something valuable, such as a hoard of Roman coins that Michael Wren didn't know about.

He would sell them to her for, say, a couple of pounds – "Glad to get rid of 'em!" – whereupon Harriet would go rushing off to the nearest museum, who would give her a thousand pounds on the spot, and loads more later on, so that she could buy all the super de luxe trainers that she wanted.

There weren't any Roman coins today, but what there was was a box of old slides with a label saying

GENUINE
"WHAT THE BUTLER SAW"
£10

Harriet's heart began to beat a little faster. All she needed were some slides and her dad's projector ...

"You didn't ought to be looking at those," said Michael Wren. "They're saucy ones, those are."

"Are they interesting?" said Harriet.

Michael Wren closed one eye in a wink. "I'll say!"

"Would people pay to come and see them, do you think?"

"You'd better believe it!"

"They're very expensive," said Harriet. She knew you always had to bargain with people in the market. You had to try and knock their prices down.

"Expensive?" said Michael Wren. He sounded indignant. "Dirt cheap, they are! That's 'cause they're not quite a full set. If they was a full set, you'd be paying a darn sight more. But seeing as they're not, I'm prepared to drop the price a little."

"How much?" said Harriet.

"Nine pounds, take it or leave it."

Harriet wondered if there was any chance of beating him down to a three pound book token and a tube of twenty-pence pieces. She decided, glumly, that there wasn't.

"I'll have to see if I can raise the money," she said. "Could you keep them for me?"

"I'll hold 'em till midday tomorrow. Not a

second longer."

"All right," said Harriet. "I'll be back!"

Tomorrow was Saturday, when Professor de Vere was coming. He was arriving at lunch time, to eat his egg plants and his passion fruits, then he was going off with Mum and Dad to the church hall to do his lecture.

Then he was coming back to drink all his whisky and sherry and spend the night under his new duvet cover before taking the train back to London. (He couldn't drive a car because of being nervous of technology.)

Harriet went scuttling off to Stinky Allport's. Stinky, like Harriet, was always looking for ways of making money.

"I've had this brilliant idea!" said Harriet.

"What?"

Stinky looked at her, guardedly. He'd had experience of Harriet's brilliant ideas. They might *sound* brilliant, in theory, but in practice they never quite seemed to work out that way.

"We get these slides," said Harriet, "and we borrow my dad's projector – "

Stinky listened, and said that he was willing to put up "two pounds and no more".

Now Harriet had two pounds, plus a tube of twenty-pence pieces, plus a three pound book token which she could sell to her mum.

She only needed another couple of pounds. Surely she could manage to raise those?

Harriet went on up the road to see Wendy Williams.

"I've had this brilliant idea," said Harriet.

Wendy said it could be as brilliant as brilliant, it wasn't any use coming to her.

"My mum's stopped my pocket money. I've only got eighty pence."

"That'll do," said Harriet. Every little helped. "I'll try Salim."

She marched on round the corner and up the hill to the new estate.

"I've had this brill..."

"Forget it," said Salim.

"Pardon?" said Harriet.

"Not interested. Not if it means money." Salim's eyes gleamed. "I'm saving up for a new video game!"

"Well, this is it," said Harriet. "I'm saving up for some new trainers. But I've had this truly brilliant idea! What we do, we buy these slides…"

Salim said he would put in a pound. "It's all I can afford to risk."

Harriet went back home to count her money: two pounds from Stinky, one pound from Salim, eighty pence from Wendy, three

pounds for the book token, two pounds forty in twenty-pence pieces.

Nine pounds twenty! Hurray! She could afford to buy the slides and still have twenty pence left in her tube. She decided that she would go straight to the market after breakfast.

She went downstairs to sell her book token to her mum. Harriet's mum was in the kitchen, drinking coffee with her friend Mrs Wheeler. Mrs Wheeler also belonged to the history society.

As Harriet entered the kitchen she heard Mrs Wheeler say, "Apparently he's so boring that half the audience fell asleep. One man even starting snoring."

"Oh, this is dreadful!" cried Harriet's mum. "Why ever did we invite him?"

"It was Grace's idea."

"Didn't she know?"

"Nobody knew! But then I got talking to this person and she told me... They had him down in Dorchester and it was simply frightful!"

"Tony will go mad." (Tony was Harriet's dad.)

"So will Henry." (Henry was Mrs Wheeler's husband.)

Harriet's mum heaved a sigh. Mrs Wheeler heaved another one.

"I thought it seemed too good to be true... someone willing to travel all the way from London for nothing but expenses."

"Now we know why."

Harriet pulled out a chair and knelt on it, elbows on the table.

"Is this the Professor?"

"Yes," said her mum, "But don't tell your dad!"

"I thought he sounded boring," said Harriet.

"I thought he sounded absolutely fascinating!" Harriet's mum looked pleadingly at Mrs Wheeler. "What about the slides? Surely they must be interesting?"

"Not according to this person. According to her he says things like, 'This is what you might see if you'd looked into the servants' hall'. Then he shows an old photograph of servants sitting round a table, cleaning cutlery. She said the photographs were so dark you couldn't see very much anyway."

"Oh, what have we let ourselves in for?" moaned Harriet's mum.

My slides won't be like that, thought Harriet. Her slides were saucy; Michael Wren had said so.

Next morning, Harriet took the bus into town. First of all she went to look at her trainers and check they were still there (they were) and then she went down the market to find Michael Wren.

"Oh, so you've come back, have you? That's a surprise," said Michael Wren. "I never thought the day would come when you'd stop fingering the goods and actually produce some hard cash! OK. Let's see the colour of your money."

Harriet handed over her nine pounds. Michael Wren handed over the box of slides.

"I hope they're good," said Harriet.

"They're good, all right! Just don't get on my case if your mum takes them off you."

"Why should she?" said Harriet.

Michael Wren said nothing: just tapped a finger to the side of his nose.

"Don't you come grizzling back to me," he said.

"I don't *grizzle*," said Harriet.

When Harriet arrived home, Professor de Vere was there. He was in the sitting room with Dad. Harriet heard his voice, high and fluting.

"The train was running approximately three minutes late... I tell a lie! It was nearer four. I checked my watch most carefully against the station clock. Four minutes late as we left Paddington. And no explanation! There never is, of course. I find nothing more irritating than being left in ignorance. A simple exercise in customer relations, that is all it takes. Just a simple exercise..."

Harriet deposited her box of slides in the hall, next to the Professor's. She was about to investigate the Professor's box, to see if his slides were as boring as Mrs Wheeler had claimed, when her dad shot out of the sitting room and almost tripped over her. He had a glazed expression on his face.

"Oh, ah, Harriet!" he said. "What are you doing? Don't touch things. Go in there and –

um – keep the Professor entertained until lunch is ready."

The Professor was an extremely long, thin man with long, thin hair that grew all round the edge of his head but not on the top. The top was smooth and shiny, like a billiard ball. Harriet wondered if he polished it every day with furniture polish.

Professor de Vere seemed uncomfortable in Harriet's presence. He sat in silence as she prattled – Harriet's idea of entertaining being to talk non-stop – and was obviously relieved when Harriet's mum appeared with the egg plants and avocados.

"Ah! Sustenance," he said.

Over lunch, the Professor told Mum about his train being four minutes late as it left Paddington.

By the end of lunch, Mum also had a glazed expression on her face. (Harriet kept herself amused by staring at the smooth bald top of the Professor's head.)

The lecture was to last from four o'clock till six. At half-past three, they set out for the church hall.

Harriet went with them as far as Stinky's house. She carried her box of slides. Stinky was going to be really pleased with them!

Harriet had said to Lynn, after lunch, "I've bought some slides. They're called 'What the Butler saw'."

Lynn had looked at her through narrowed eyes.

"You filthy little beast!" she said. "It'll be all dirty pictures!"

"*Will* it?" said Harriet.

"Well, of course it will! It's what nasty old men used to put pennies into slot machines for."

"So they could see the dirty pictures?"

"*Yes*," said Lynn. "You ought to be ashamed of yourself!"

"I didn't know they were dirty," said Harriet.

"So what did you think they were?"

"Just pictures of food and stuff."

Food on the table. With sauce. Saucy, like Michael Wren had said.

"You're pathetic," said Lynn.

Harriet didn't see there was anything

pathetic about making money. She bet she had her trainers before Lynn had her ice skates!

Harriet and Stinky went down to the far end of Stinky's garden so that they could hold the slides up to the light and see the dirty pictures without Stinky's mum or dad coming to ask them what they were doing.

"Let's have a look, let's have a look!"

Stinky jostled Harriet for possession of the box.

"I was the one that found them," said Harriet. "I bags look first!"

She took one out and squinted at it.

"What is it?" said Stinky. "Is it a naked lady?"

"It's a – an empty room," said Harriet. "I think."

It was a bit too dark to be sure, but she certainly couldn't see any naked ladies.

"Try the next one!" said Stinky.

They tried the next one, and the next one, and the one after that.

"They've got to be somewhere!" cried Stinky.

They looked and they looked, but they couldn't find a naked lady anywhere. All there were were lots of people dressed up as servants.

Servants washing up, servants scrubbing floors, servants lighting fires, servants sitting round a table cleaning cutlery...

Harriet swallowed. "I think something's gone a bit wrong," she said.

"You're telling me!" shouted Stinky. "You've been done! This is *rubbish*! I want my two pounds back!"

"I want my slides back!"

Harriet bundled all the boring servants into their box.

"Don't worry," she said. "We'll make far more than two pounds once I've got the right ones back!"

Harriet ran as fast as her legs would carry her to the church hall. As she burst in through the main door she bumped into a group of people coming out.

"Disgusting!" they were saying. "Absolutely disgusting!"

Inside the entrance was a large sign

which read:

LIFE BELOW STAIRS
LECTURE & SLIDE SHOW
BY PROFESSOR DE VERE
THIS WAY ⟶

Harriet followed the arrow until she came to another sign. This one said:

LECTURE
IN HERE

Harriet eased open the door and crept in. She was just in time to hear the Professor's high, fluty voice.

"This is what you might have seen if you had looked into the servants' hall."

On the screen appeared a picture of a plump lady wearing frilly bloomers. The picture wobbled slightly because Harriet's dad, who was operating the projector, was bent double, clutching at his stomach.

Harriet thought at first that he was in pain, but then a loud trumpeting noise burst from him and she realised that he was laughing.

Other people were also laughing, but rather more discreetly, making little squeaks and choking noises into their handkerchieves. Harriet could see her mum and Mrs Wheeler, their hands clamped to their mouths.

"And this," droned the Professor, "is the view inside the butler's pantry."

Harriet's eyes grew wide. A naked lady! A woman sitting nearby stuffed her handkerchief into her mouth; another, unable to control herself, staggered to her feet and made for the door. Small chirruping sounds were coming from her.

Harriet's mum suddenly turned and caught sight of Harriet.

"Harriet," she said weakly, "what are you doing here?"

Harriet didn't like to say that she had come for her slides; it didn't seem quite the right moment. She went back outside, into the sunshine.

The chirruping lady was there. She was leaning against a wall, gasping. She took one look at Harriet and erupted.

"Oh, dear! Oh, heavens! Oh, my goodness!"

The chirruping lady tottered off down the path. Harriet went to sit on a tombstone and wait.

She had only been waiting a few minutes when the door burst open and the Professor appeared. Harriet jumped up.

"Excuse me," she said, holding out her box. "I think that these are yours and…"

She got no further. With a strangulated yelp, the Professor snatched the box from her.

"What about mine?" cried Harriet; but the Professor had gone.

Harriet's slides were still in the hall – and if she knew anything about grown-ups they wouldn't be returned to her.

Now what was she going to do? No slides, no money –

"Ah, Harriet!" Harriet's dad had appeared, wiping his eyes with his handkerchief. "Fancy seeing you here! Have you come to nag me again about your fancy trainers?"

"Um – " said Harriet.

"How much were they? Forty pounds?"

"Fifty to *begin* with," said Harriet, "but then they put the price down. Then I..."

"Here!"

Harriet watched in amazement as her dad took out his wallet and peeled off four ten-pound notes.

"Take it! I'm feeling generous. I haven't enjoyed myself so much in years. Laugh? I nearly split my sides!"

Harriet's dad reeled off, clutching at his ribs. Harriet stared down, thoughtfully, at her four ten-pound notes.

That was thirty-five pounds for trainers, two pounds for Stinky, one pound for Salim, eighty pence for Wendy – and one pound twenty left over. Hooray!

Harriet turned and ran. If she went like the wind she might just reach the shoe shop before it closed.

HARRIET AND THE HOUND FROM HELL

"I wish I could have a dog," said Harriet.

Harriet was always wishing she could have a dog – and her mum was always telling her that she couldn't.

"What about Fat Cat?"

"Fat Cat wouldn't mind. He *likes* dogs."

Fat Cat, sitting on top of the kitchen cupboard, opened one eye and closed it again. Dogs were rubbish. Dogs were scum!

"See?" said Harriet. "He's not frightened."

"I don't care; you're not having one. I know what would happen if you had a dog."

"What?" said Harriet.

"You'd get bored and wouldn't exercise it.

It would be left to me."

"No, it wouldn't!" Harriet was indignant. "I'd walk it *every day*. I'd take it up the park and we'd play together."

"Oh, yes?" said her mum.

"I would," said Harriet. She opened her dog book that she had borrowed from the library.

The dog book had pictures of every single breed of dog known to man or woman. Harriet pointed wistfully at a picture of a Great Dane.

"That's the sort of dog I'd like."

"No way!" said her mum.

Harriet flicked over the pages.

"That one?"

Her mum looked.

"We are not," she said, "having a thing that size in the house."

Harriet sighed. She liked St Bernards.

"What about a wolfhound?"

"Certainly not."

"Afghan?"

"Harriet, I've already told you – we are not having any dog."

"Yorkshire terrier!" roared Harriet.

"I said *any* dog."

"Well, I wouldn't want a Yorkshire terrier, anyway."

Harriet closed the book with a bang. She wanted a big dog. A real dog. Not some silly little niminy piminy thing with a bow in its hair.

Cousin Birdie had a Yorkshire terrier that wore a bow in its hair. It was called Poochie, and next weekend it was coming to stay while Cousin Birdie went off to London.

Cousin Birdie was old and rather peculiar. She had once had an entire houseful of Yorkshire terriers with bows in their hair.

She showed them at dog shows, where she sometimes won rosettes and quarrelled fiercely with the judges when she didn't. Judges, according to Cousin Birdie, were biased. (Biased meant giving rosettes to other people's Yorkshire terriers instead of Cousin Birdie's.)

A woman called Maude Ffinch was her particular rival. Cousin Birdie was extremely jealous of Maude Ffinch because Maude Ffinch's Yorkshire terriers had won more

rosettes than hers.

Now Cousin Birdie only had Poochie; but Poochie, she assured Mum, was going to be a champion.

"He'll beat Maude Ffinch's tatty little beast into a cocked hat. That'll show her! Thinks she's the queen bee, her and her *Laddy Boy*." Cousin Birdie's lip curled into a hoop. "Laddy Boy! I ask you!"

Harriet couldn't really see that Laddy Boy was any worse than Poochie Poochie

(Poochie Poochie of Glenmore was his official name) but you couldn't ever say anything like that to Cousin Birdie. She would brook no criticism.

"Poochie Poochie is going to win *first* prize, and Maude Ffinch is going to come absolutely *nowhere*!"

The dog show was being held only a few days after Poochie's stay with Harriet and her family, so Cousin Birdie was naturally anxious that every care should be taken of him.

"*No* naughty walkies in the muddy parkie. *No* naughty playing in the muddy garden. Just walky walkies on the lead around the nice clean streets. And no talky talkies with other doggies, please!"

"Doesn't he like to talk to other dogs?" said Harriet.

"Poochie is a *house* dog; he doesn't care to mix. In fact, if you had a nice cat litter tray..."

There was a pause. Fat Cat, sitting on his elbows on top of the television, gazed down upon Poochie with silent contempt. Cat litter tray! He hadn't used a cat litter tray since he was a tiny kitten.

"There really wouldn't be any need for him to go out at all," said Cousin Birdie.

"Oh, but surely," said Mum, "he'll get smelly if he doesn't go out?"

"Not if he's groomed properly. I've brought all his brushes and combs."

Mum said quickly, "Harriet can groom him."

Cousin Birdie swivelled her big marbly eyes in Harriet's direction.

"He needs grooming at least twice a day, Harriet, or his coat will become matted."

Harriet looked at Poochie's coat. It was long and silky and hung down to the ground. On top of his head, his hair was tied into a bunch with a red ribbon.

"I think it'd be easier just to take him for a walk," she said.

"I insist that he is groomed!" cried Cousin Birdie. "I can't possibly leave him with you if you're not going to groom him!"

"Harriet will groom him." Mum said it soothingly, with a warning glance at Harriet.

Mum had a soft spot for Cousin Birdie. She said that she was eccentric but harmless.

"Don't worry about Poochie. We'll look after him."

Looking after Poochie turned out to be a full-time job. As well as all his brushes and combs, Cousin Birdie had brought his own special dog bed with its own special blanket, his eating bowl, his drinking bowl, his tins of special dog food, his vitamin tablets, his conditioning tablets, and his special low-fat milk.

There was a long list of feeding instructions – "He needs his food at regular intervals during the day, and please make sure it's mixed properly, in the right proportions" – and an extra set of ribbons for his top knot, "because I like him to have a change of ribbon every day."

Mum said that Harriet could see to Poochie's breakfast and to his elevenses and to his lunch and to his tea and his dinner and his supper. She said that she would see to his ribbons.

"I think that's a fair division of labour,

don't you?" She smiled happily at Harriet. "After all, you're the one who wants a dog."

Not a dog like *this*, thought Harriet.

It was difficult to think of Poochie as a dog at all. The only dog-like thing he did was bark, which he did practically non-stop until even Harriet, who was generally quite fond of a bit of noise, felt like screaming.

"It's because he's not exercised enough," said Mum; but she wouldn't let Harriet take him in the garden and play with him for fear he'd get dirty.

"Then what are we going to do?" cried Harriet.

"I suppose you could try him with a ball," said Mum. "So long as you don't get him over-excited. He's probably not used to playing. We don't want him having a fit."

Poochie was so unused to playing that he didn't even know how to.

Harriet tried rolling the ball and throwing the ball; she tried lying on her back and making doggy noises. She tried running around the room and crawling on all fours.

Poochie just sat and looked at her.

"I think he must be a bit simple," said
Harriet.

"He's not simple," said Mum. "He's just
never learnt. It's because he's a show dog."

Harriet felt sorry for Poochie, being a show
dog. What kind of life was it if you never
learnt how to play or run about? If you were
never allowed to go for walks or talk to other
dogs?

"He must be really bored," she said.

"Maybe he enjoys it," said Mum, but she
didn't sound very convinced.

When Dad came home that evening he said, "Aha! The hound from hell! Have to be careful with that one - tear your throat out as soon as look at you."

"He would not!" Harriet said it indignantly. She and Poochie were getting on quite well.

She had fed him all his meals and groomed his coat, twice, and he had been as good as gold. Once he had even licked her hand. It had made Harriet feel almost fond of him.

"Dad's only joking," said Mum.

"I don't think you ought to joke about Poochie," said Harriet. "He has a very sad life."

"Sad life?" said Dad. "Who are you kidding? I've never known such a pampered beast!"

"He'd far rather be outside, playing with the other dogs," said Harriet.

"Ah, well, that's the price you pay for beating Maude Ffinch into a cocked hat!"

"Nobody asked *him* if he wanted to beat Maude Ffinch!" cried Harriet. "I don't think it's fair!"

"Life isn't," said Dad.

When Lynn came in she said, "Ugh! So it's here, is it? Yappy, smelly creature!"

Harriet couldn't in truth deny that Poochie was yappy, but she rose up strongly at the suggestion that he smelt.

"I've groomed him twice! He smells *beautiful*!" And she caught him up and buried her nose in his silky fur to prove the point.

"He'd look a whole lot better," said Lynn, "if he were clipped."

Harriet secretly agreed with this. If all his ridiculous hair were taken off, then maybe Poochie could start to be a real dog.

"Poor Poochie," she said. She bent her head and whispered in his ear: "Maybe I'll take you for a walk tomorrow, if it stops raining."

It rained all of Saturday and all of Sunday. Poochie stayed indoors (except for just going into the back garden when he absolutely had to), being groomed and eating his food at regular intervals, and barking.

It wasn't until Monday that the rain

stopped. Fortunately, as it was the summer holidays, Harriet didn't have to go to school.

"Can I take Poochie for a walk?" she said to her mum.

Mum glanced anxiously out of the window.

"It's all right," said Harriet. "It's dry as dry."

"Well, keep to the roads," said Mum, "and don't let him sniff anything or talk to other dogs. And for goodness' sake don't get him dirty! Remember, Cousin Birdie's coming back this afternoon."

Harriet fetched Poochie's lead. Unlike normal dogs, he didn't jump up and down or start turning in circles. He didn't seem to know what a lead was for.

"Walkies!" said Harriet; but Poochie just looked at her.

Determinedly, she led him out through the front gate. Where should they go? Harriet decided that they would walk up the road towards the park.

They wouldn't go *into* the park; but at least Poochie could stand by the gates and look at all the grass and the trees and the other dogs enjoying themselves.

On the way there, they bumped into Stinky Allport carrying his football.

"What's that?" said Stinky, pointing at Poochie.

"It's my dog," said Harriet.

"Dog?" said Stinky. "Call that a dog?"

"Well, it's not actually mine," said Harriet. "But it's a good dog."

Stinky bounced his football. "What's it called?"

Harriet hesitated. "Tiger," she said.

"*Tiger?*"

"'Cause he's actually very fierce. I know he doesn't look it, but he is. He's a hound from hell," said Harriet.

"Oh, yeah?" said Stinky.

"He is so!" said Harriet.

Stinky plainly wasn't convinced. He eyed Poochie contemptuously.

"My aunt's got a German shepherd," he said.

"He'd see off a German shepherd any day! German shepherd's nothing to him."

They reached the gates of the park.

"Coming in, then?" said Stinky.

Harriet shook her head. "I can't," she said. "I'm -"

She was about to say she wasn't allowed to get Poochie in a mess.

She stopped.

"What's the problem?" jeered Stinky. "Scared he might get ate up by other dogs?"

"It's not that," said Harriet. "I'm scared he might attack them. I know he's only small, but he goes for the legs."

She gazed down at Poochie, on the end of his lead. For the first time since he had come to them, he was looking almost like a real dog. His ears were up, his eyes were bright, his nose was twitching.

"I suppose I could just walk him on the path," she said.

Harriet and Stinky, with Poochie on his lead, walked into the park and set off along the path. They had only gone a few yards when from out of nowhere an enormous black dog appeared. It was about twenty times the size of Poochie: it was almost the size of Harriet.

Its head was bigger by far than Stinky's football – and it was making straight for them, snorting and roaring, at the speed of an express train!

"Run for it!" yelled Stinky.

Stinky legged it to the nearest tree. Harriet bent to snatch up Poochie, but before she could do so the big black dog was upon them.

Harriet froze. The dog put its head down to sniff at Poochie's backside. Poochie sprang round. He bared his teeth and made a noise that sounded to Harriet like swearing.

The big black dog didn't stay to argue: it turned and bolted, its stumpy tail between its legs.

"Phew!" said Harriet.

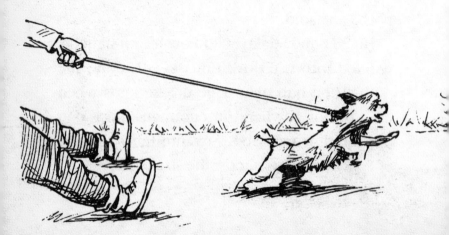

"Has it gone?" Stinky emerged cautiously from behind his tree. "You know what that was? That was a Rottweiler, that was!"

A Rottweiler! And Poochie had seen it off!

"Told you he was fierce," said Harriet. She patted Poochie's top knot. "Good dog!"

"I thought it best to keep away," explained Stinky. "They manage better on their own."

Poochie had certainly managed on his own. Harriet felt quite proud of him.

"You gonna let him off?" said Stinky.

Harriet wrestled with her conscience. Her mum had said not to; Cousin Birdie had said not to; but what harm could it do?

He wasn't going to go anywhere. All he was going to do was just walk along the path with Harriet and Stinky.

"All right," said Harriet. She unclipped Poochie's lead.

"Heel!" she said. "Good dog!"

Poochie didn't know about "heel". He had never in his life before been let off the lead... he had never in his life before seen so much open space!

He took one look, spotted a puddle of mud, and dived joyfully towards it.

"Hoy!" shrieked Harriet. "Get out of there!"

She might as well have saved her breath. Poochie was in ecstasy. He was rolling on his back, to and fro, to and fro, in the lovely squidgy, slushy mud. He was being a dog at last! A real dog!

"Cripes," said Harriet, as the black stinking mess that was Poochie hauled itself out of the puddle.

Poochie shook himself vigorously, scraped the ground with his front paws and went tearing off across the grass in pursuit of a German shepherd dog.

"Stop him!" yelled Stinky. "It'll eat him alive!"

Harriet and Stinky went tearing off in pursuit.

Too late! By the time they arrived an outraged owner was hauling at the German shepherd's collar and making furious shooshing motions at Poochie.

"Do you mind getting your dog away from my bitch?" yelled the owner.

Poochie didn't want to come away from the German shepherd; he had obviously taken a fancy to her.

"Right little goer, isn't he?" Stinky said it admiringly. "Let's teach him to play football."

Now that he was off the lead, Poochie was a different dog. He soon picked up the idea of playing football. They had a wonderful game all across the park, with Harriet and Stinky passing the ball and Poochie doing his best to intercept.

Then they reached the woody bit, where there were squirrels to chase and undergrowth to explore. Poochie's red ribbon disappeared, and he got burrs and bits of leaf and twig all tangled up in his lovely silky coat, which actually wasn't lovely and silky any more but filthy and matted.

Harriet regarded him in dismay. This was the dog that was going to beat Maude Ffinch and her Laddy Boy into a cocked hat!

"A dirty dog is a happy dog," said Stinky, who by this time was rather dirty himself.

Poochie stood panting, looking up at them, bright-eyed, through a fringe of hair.

"I dunno what Mum's going to say," worried Harriet. She took out her handkerchief to try and wipe off some of the mud, but by now it had dried as hard as rock cake.

"I know!" shouted Stinky. "He can go and swim in the lake!"

Poochie liked swimming in the lake. In

fact he liked it so much that he refused to come out and Harriet and Stinky had to wade in after him.

All three of them emerged covered in duckweed and green slime. Poochie looked worse than ever.

Oh, well, thought Harriet; it was only a bit of mud. It would wash out. They could use Lynn's special shampoo and conditioner, and then dry him with Lynn's hair dryer and get him all silky again before Cousin Birdie turned up. She would never need to know.

As they ambled back down the path, with Stinky and Harriet idly kicking the football and Poochie making little forays on to the grass to investigate interesting smells, a big tweedy woman came striding towards them with another Yorkshire terrier. This one had a blue bow in its top knot.

Blue bow took one look at Poochie and flew at him, frothing with rage. As Harriet said afterwards, it wasn't Poochie's fault. He had been quietly minding his own business, sniffing at a smell. But naturally, if a dog jumps you, you have to defend yourself.

Poochie defended himself vigorously.

The tweedy woman bawled, "Get him off! Get him off! Before he marks him!"

Harriet made a grab at some flying fur: the woman snatched it from her.

"Laddy Boy! My poor Laddy Boy! What did the nasty vicious doggie do to you?"

So that was Laddy Boy, was it? The famous Laddy Boy that Poochie was going to beat into a cocked hat.

"Mine didn't do anything," said Harriet. "It was yours that started it."

"How *dare* you!" said the woman. "My Laddy Boy wouldn't harm a flea."

"Ought to be locked up," muttered Harriet, as she and Stinky went on their way, with Poochie safely back on the lead.

"Poochie didn't do a *thing*," she crooned, "*did* you?"

"Didn't stand a chance," said Stinky. He studied Poochie a moment. "Looks to me," he said, "as if it's gone and ate a bit of his ear."

"*What?*" Harriet dropped to her knees beside Poochie.

She gave a wail. It was true! The tip of

one of Poochie's ears was missing!

"But it's all right," said Stinky, "'cause ours came away with a mouthful of fur, so I reckon they was quits."

Poochie stepped out on the way home like a dog who is not so much quits as positively triumphant. He swaggered, he pranced, he puffed himself up.

He had seen off a Rottweiler, made overtures to a German shepherd, rolled in the mud, swum in the lake, and had a punch-up with the hated Laddy Boy. What more could a dog desire?

Poochie was in his seventh heaven of bliss – but Cousin Birdie was not going to be. Nor was Harriet's mum.

Harriet's mum was going to go raving mad. She would stop Harriet's pocket money, for sure.

"Maybe…" Stinky bounced his football. "Maybe you could tell 'em –"

"What?" said Harriet.

"I dunno," said Stinky. He paused, at his front gate. "See you tomorrow?"

"Don't expect so," said Harriet. "Don't

expect I'll be let go anywhere tomorrow. Expect I'll be shut up in my room eating bread and water."

Harriet had done some dreadful things in her time. She had locked the headmaster in the gardening shed; she had put a red T-shirt into the washing machine and dyed all the sheets and pillow cases in streaky shades of pink; she had set fire to the back fence; she had cut a hole in the carpet – but none of it was as bad as letting Cousin Birdie's prize Yorkie get the tip of his ear bitten off.

Now she was going to be for it!

She smuggled Poochie in through the back gate, hoping that at least she might be able to dump him in the sink and wash away the mud before Mum caught sight of him.

Maybe if he was all silky and brushed nobody would notice the tip of his ear. After all, it was only a very *tiny* piece of ear.

She pushed open the kitchen door and lifted Poochie to put him in the sink. There was a screech. Harriet spun round in alarm. Cousin Birdie was standing there!

"What have you done with my Poochie?"

screamed Cousin Birdie.

Just Harriet's luck! Cousin Birdie had come back earlier than expected.

Needless to say, she noticed the ear immediately. She noticed the ear almost even before she noticed the mud.

That was it, she said. The dog was ruined. He was never going to beat Maude Ffinch into a cocked hat now. Harriet might just as well take him away and – and give him to the first person she saw!

Harriet was shocked. Give him away? Give Poochie away? Just because a tiny piece of his ear was missing? She'd never heard such wickedness!

"Well, he's no use to me," said Cousin Birdie.

Mum, doing her best, said that of course she and Dad would buy Cousin Birdie a replacement. But Cousin Birdie said she didn't want another one, thank you very much; Poochie was the last of a line.

If Mum and Dad felt guilty, they could buy her some tomato plants, instead. She was going to take up market gardening. She had

had enough of dog shows: she was sick of all the jealousy and pettiness that went on.

"That Maude Ffinch and her precious Laddy Boy. Let her win first prize! See if I care!"

"I don't think she will win first prize," said Harriet, running water into the sink. "I don't think she'll win any sort of prize. Poochie pulled a lump of Laddy Boy's fur out."

Cousin Birdie's face lit up.

"Did he really?" she said. "How utterly splendid!"

When Cousin Birdie went home next day, she left Poochie in Harriet's care.

"He's yours," she said, "if you want him."

Harriet turned breathlessly to her mum.

"Mum," she said. "*Can* I?"

Mum just humped a shoulder.

Fat Cat, curled into a ball in Poochie's basket, opened one eye and twitched a whisker. That dog had better behave itself!

After lunch, a new-look, bristle-cut Poochie, minus his top knot and red ribbon, strode purposefully up the road with Harriet.

At the gates to the park they met Stinky and Wendy Williams.

"What's that?" said Wendy, pointing.

"This is my dog," said Harriet.

"Dog?" said Wendy. "Call that a dog?"

"Hound from hell," said Stinky. "Sees off Rottweilers... that's a good dog, that is! Hey, Tiger!"

He bent and snapped his fingers.

"How about a game of football?"

DIMANCHE DILLER

by Henrietta Branford

When Dimanche is orphaned at the tender age of one, Chief Inspector Barry Bullpit advertises for any known relative to come forward. Unluckily for Dimanche, her real aunt does not see the message – but a bogus one does! So Dimanche, who is heir to an enormous fortune, is sent to live with the dreaded Valburga Vilemile, who tries to rid herself of Dimanche at every opportunity. Her lack of success owes itself to Polly Pugh, who looks after Dimanche, foils all attempts to polish her off, and helps her find her true aunt.

In 1995, *Dimanche Diller* won the Smarties 7-9 category Fiction Award, a prize awarded for the year's most exciting piece of children's fiction.

£2.99

KING HENRY VIII'S SHOES
by Karen Wallace

When Catherine finds a beautiful golden box in the maze at Hampton Court, little does she realise that it contains a shoe belonging to none other than King Henry VIII of England! And she is even more surprised when that larger-than-life monarch from Tudor times comes back – to twentieth-century England – to find his shoe. Catherine and her class mates learn all about Henry VIII and he finds out that in the twentieth century, kings can go shopping, go to burger bars and even ride on a bus!

£2.99

Order Form

To order direct from the publishers, just make a list of the titles you want and fill in the form below:

Name ....

Address ....

....

....

Send to: Dept 6, HarperCollins Publishers Ltd, Westerhill Road, Bishopbriggs, Glasgow G64 2QT.

Please enclose a cheque or postal order to the value of the cover price, plus:

UK & BFPO: Add £1.00 for the first book, and 25p per copy for each addition book ordered.

Overseas and Eire: Add £2.95 service charge. Books will be sent by surface mail but quotes for airmail despatch will be given on request.

A 24-hour telephone ordering service is available to Visa and Access card holders: 0141-772 2281